LITTLE TREE

e.e. cummings

LITTLE TREE

illustrated by Deborah Kogan Ray

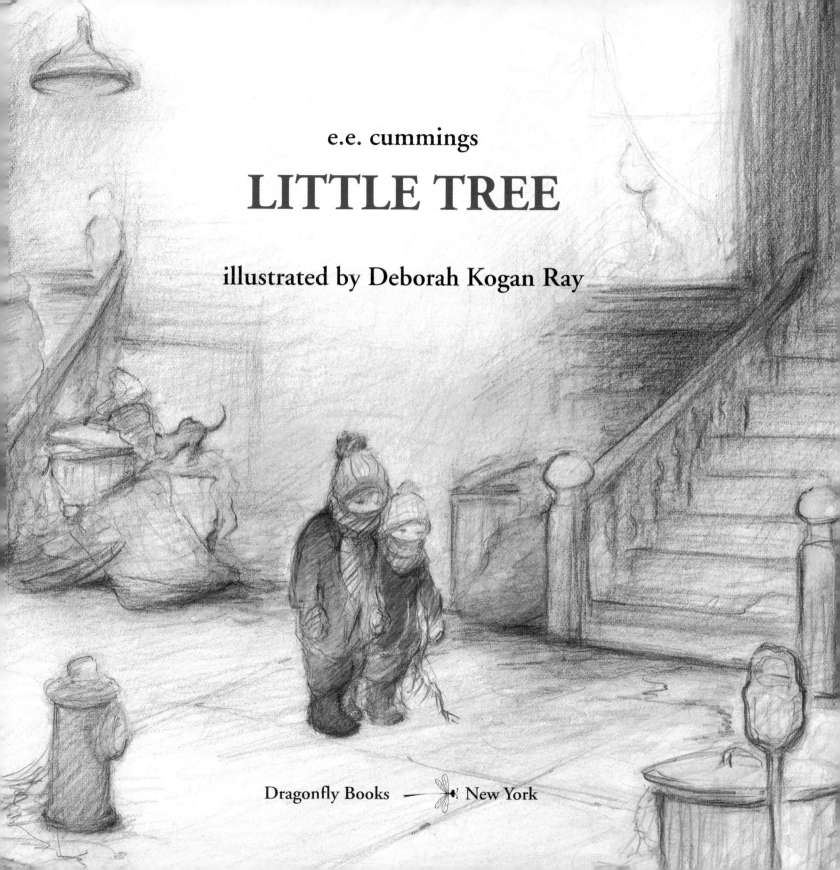

Dragonfly Books — New York

To Barbara and Clarke
many Christmases
many little trees

Text copyright © 1923, 1925, renewed 1951, 1953 by e.e. cummings. Copyright © 1973, 1976 by the Trustees for the e.e. cummings Trust. Copyright © 1973, 1976 by George James Firmage. Illustrations copyright © 1987 by Deborah Kogan.

All rights reserved. Published in the United States by Dragonfly Books, an imprint of Random House Children's Books, a division of Random House, Inc., New York. Originally published in hardcover by Crown Publishers, an imprint of Random House Children's Books, a division of Random House, Inc., New York, in 1987.

Dragonfly Books with the colophon is a registered trademark of Random House, Inc.

Visit us on the Web! www.randomhouse.com/kids

Educators and librarians, for a variety of teaching tools, visit us at www.randomhouse.com/teachers

The Library of Congress has cataloged the hardcover edition of this work as follows:
cummings, e.e. (Edward Estlin). Little tree.
Summary: The poet/individualist's ode to a small tree decorated for Christmas
and proud to receive admiring attention.
ISBN 978-0-517-56598-8 (trade)
1. Christmas trees—Juvenile poetry. 2. Children's poetry, America. [1. Christmas trees—Poetry. 2. American poetry.]
I. Ray, Deborah, ill. II. Title.
PS3505.U334L5 1987   811'.52   86030940

ISBN 978-0-517-88178-1 (pbk.)

MANUFACTURED IN CHINA

11 10 9 8 7 6 5 4

Random House Children's Books supports the First Amendment and celebrates the right to read.

little tree
little silent Christmas tree
you are so little
you are more like a flower

who found you in the green forest
and were you very sorry to come away?

see   i will comfort you
because you smell so sweetly

i will kiss your cool bark
and hug you safe and tight
just as your mother would,
only don't be afraid

look   the spangles
that sleep all the year in a dark box
dreaming of being taken out and allowed to shine,

the balls the chains red and gold the fluffy threads,

put up your little arms
and i'll give them all to you to hold
every finger shall have its ring
and there won't be a single place dark or unhappy

then when you're quite dressed
you'll stand in the window for everyone to see
and how they'll stare!
oh but you'll be very proud

and my little sister and i will take hands
and looking up at our beautiful tree
we'll dance and sing
"Noel Noel"

little tree
little silent Christmas tree
you are so little
you are more like a flower

who found you in the green forest
and were you very sorry to come away?
see   i will comfort you
because you smell so sweetly

i will kiss your cool bark
and hug you safe and tight
just as your mother would,
only don't be afraid

look   the spangles
that sleep all the year in a dark box
dreaming of being taken out and allowed to shine,
the balls the chains red and gold the fluffy threads,

put up your little arms
and i'll give them all to you to hold
every finger shall have its ring
and there won't be a single place dark or unhappy

then when you're quite dressed
you'll stand in the window for everyone to see
and how they'll stare!
oh but you'll be very proud

and my little sister and i will take hands
and looking up at our beautiful tree
we'll dance and sing
"Noel Noel"